Poetry

by

Micheal Hopkins

Copyright © 2017 by Micheal Hopkins

Shywind Creations, Micheal Hopkins
micheal@shywindcreations.com

Ordering Information:
Quantity sales. Special discounts are available on quantity purchases by corporations, associations, and others. For details, contact the publisher at the address above. Printed in the United States of America.

Poetry by Micheal Hopkins

Poet-Micheal Hopkins and his wife Carol-Artist

Life is a garden and each man is given his pick of one perfect rose,
and you are mine. Love Wind

CONTENTS

DEDICATION

To my loving wife, Carol that has been my inspiration for all things in my life. My Dear friend David, my children for making me crazy, and to the many people in my life who encouraged me to tell the Ancient Warrior's story.

ACKNOWLEDGMENTS

To my lovely wife, Carol, without her drive and determination my poetry would never have left my mind or my computer.

Thank you, Carol, for the photographs and art.

To the veterans of all conflicts friend and foe alike.

Introduction

The Ancient Warrior is a composite of many lives in many times just as this book is a compilation of his previous stories. Over the years, it has become hard to discern where my life experiences leave off and the Ancient Warrior's begin. I hope you will enjoy this book and learn from my Ancient Warrior, his code of honor and sense of duty that seems in such short supply now days.

My Poems are Mythical Medieval Romantic poetry. They tell the story of one warrior who over his lifetimes has followed a quest given by the gods as punishment yet also reward to find Loves Lost Tear. He can only know complete peace and rest when Loves Lost Tear is found. In his quest, he knows love but briefly he knows pain, fear, and loss intimately. His one true love is seen both as comfort and curse a source of joy and pain the reason to defy the gods and carry his battle to the very gates of hell and eternity.

The Warrior fears nothing but failure or rejection. He has traveled over times shores, been tossed on eternity's seas, warred on dragons, and daemons, and danced with the same. His memories span the great abyss of his lifetimes allowing him to continue his quest of centuries. Will he find Loves Lost Tear or will he just leave his step in the sands of time amongst the crystal shards of mans shattered dreams. Who can say?

"Emerald Tears "is a composite of many lives and fears nothing but failure or rejection by his lady. He has traveled over times shores been tossed on eternity's seas warred on dragons and daemons and danced with the same. His memories span the great abyss of his lifetimes allowing him to continue his quest of centuries. Will he find Loves Lost Tear or will he just leave his step in the sands of time amongst the crystal shards of man's shattered dreams? Who can say?

CHAPTER-1

The Ancient Warrior

The Ancient Warrior is an old soul that has lived many existences. He seeks to complete a quest given in times far distant, and different from now. The poems tell the stories of his life from before, and his visions of the next life he must endure, until he completes his quest. His stories untold until now, tell what he has seen, or endured in his travels, along the sands of time by eternities' sea.

What the author has found to be so fascinating, and exciting about the poetry he inspires, is that no two people interpret the same story the same way.

Ancient Warrior

Upon the shores, he stands, bent, scarred, and alive
His walk proud, his head crowned in snow, cascading
He sings of times long forgotten, songs of battle true
His dragon upon his left, emerald tears in the sand

Daemons march in long silent file, chasing eternity
The wind caresses the cheek, a kiss, a touch
Eternity upon time's seas, soundless in it vigil
Ancient warrior time's companion, upon these forgotten shores

Could I dance again in battle the plain crimson, fallen foe and friend
The songs in remembrance, the dance that never ends
Gods smile in silent mirth, heaven laughs in delight
Ancient warrior on the sands, dragon by his side

Time is a cruel gift, a treasure, a curse, eternity but his prison
Duty and honour, laughter and tears, the warrior presses on
A quest in search of meaning, a promise in search of time
The soul stained with crimson, tattered, frayed, and soiled

Ancient warrior stalwart friend, daemon's gift to you
Forever but an instant, a dream to see you through
Heaven's gate or hell's abyss, neither will open for you
Loves lost tear your seeking, laughter in the deep

Micheal Hopkins

Blood Shadow

I stand my take, the world at the bay, my sword held high
Would in times of wish, a desire come through, could you smile
The wild times of ever more upon the seas, or can we begin
The ride in a dragon's cart, the sounds upon the sand

I walk for in the seeking, the sands beneath my feet
The songs of other times, drive my heart and its plaintive beat
The winds of never were, the sighs of are you there
The clouds wrap the mists, in the watching god's hair

The daemons sing in silent harmony, the songs never to be heard
The leaves of times wandering dreams, the shadow of a bird
I can laugh to the reason, cry for the cause, smile to your memory
The need to caress, the touch of your soul, the heart I need to hear

Gods and daemons, imps and devils, live in dragon fear
The dragons march to bring my soul, the eternity or the plain
The sounds of songs I never heard echo in my brain
The wish of time the need of heart, the wanting to begin, the life

The steel upon my battle hand, the shield upon my arm
The lightning upon the sands of time, keep you safe from harm
The rocks are foes in silent file, the blood a shadow of then
The warrior knows no other fate, let the battle begin

Daemon's Curse

Daemon's curse, and eternity's cold winds
The dragon's fire the challenge begins
I move to the field to slay those with in
Daemon's curse, times strong tides only gods see inside

I stand on the field today the dragons daemons to slay
Will the victory fall to me or will I again face eternity
Take the step move the banner call the charge
Let the future begin, I am the warrior of flesh and steel

I stand the challenge accepted so soon
The dragons move to the fore the battle to do
Steel on scale claw in flesh the battle of self
Decided this night

Shall I stand and hold this shaky ground
Advance to the centre the dragons abound
I chose to stand and hold my place
The dragons and daemons move back a pace

Micheal Hopkins

Metals of Our Steel

Would the times, the scores of clouds, the rim of time
The moon, the stars, the smiles in the sun
The seas, the sand, the waves of time see the heavens
The dragons are in the mood or time the eternal song

Would you see in all that is here, the times in the sand
The rocks, the mountains, the skye of emerald time
The daemons will watch the angels will guard
The warrior will move to your side

The heart, the soul, the reasons of now of then
The world is a place of fickle fate and moving clouds
The earth a moment on eternity's face
The elements are all that we have, the metals of our steel

The Foe

The green hell of war, the blood, the pain
When and in what time will man learn
I was there, the pain, the times, the hurt
I was there, I am alive, they are gone

Walk in the private hell of memory
Stand on the plain of cold fury
Feel the hurt of hot pain and sodden care
I am the warrior, I am the man, I am

Would you trade the times with me
Would you learn the meaning of Honour
Can you see the flames of Valor
Will the song of Duty strike your heart

I am the warrior; I fought to die, to live
I fought to see the dragons in emerald skye
Would the time, would the place, would you see
Can you feel the time, can you feel the place

Honoured enemy, valiant foe, kinsman
We met on the field, each in honour bound
Each to stay, to live, or feed the ground
I honour you, I seek your time, I am the warrior

Walk in time and place with me, we seek
I see the honoured, the duty bound, I see
I seek those I placed upon this cold ground
I seek to honour the souls, the foes, my friends

Warrior Child

Warrior child riding times lost wind
Chasing the next to begin again
Dragon's pride Daemon's mirth
Prisoner trapped between heaven and earth

Eternity laughs seas roll in, sands and wishes
Dancing in mysts of time clouds of shadow
Chasing your dream seeking the wish
Mounting the charge on eternity's gate

Tears or smiles, laughter or dew, life the challenge
Eternity your due, Daemon fires to warm your soul
Dragon games so long ago remembering the passion
Forgetting the pain seeking the shards to build dreams again

Warrior child wild and free, whisper the name call the price
Eternity slows, seas do still, and clouds crown the warrior hill
Foeman and friend await you on the rim
The dark rim of your eternity.

He Cried

He stands and sees the skye
He wishes the world to die, he cried
The wish the sound the smile of time
The words, the lies, the heart unkind

He wishes, he smiles, he cries again
The stories the tales that never end
The truth a fragile thing, the stories the pain
He cried, she smiled, the world inside died

I was once in love so deep so true
I was once the man who made the world of you
You took, you took, and you never gave
You treated him as a lowly slave

The times, the ages, the gifts he gave
The motion of his heart the tune of the soul
The silent drums of trust long ago
You treated the soul the heart that was true

You treated them as sacrifice to the goddess of you
I gave and gave the world at your feet
I moved the heavens to cushion your feet
You took, you stole, you never gave back

The soul, the heart, the love under constant attack
You saw the power given to you, the pain the hurt
All that you would do, you struck, you poisoned, you killed it too
He cried he cried what else could he do

Changing Tide

The wish of time is in the smile the one that you give to me
The times of now are in my heart the joy for all to see
I walk upon the plains of then my past upon the rim
Gods do laugh to see me here and the games begin

Oh man of mortal pale and life, do you remember then
The warrior stands in glorious full view the battle does begin
I move in the shades of night to find the foemen true
And in the silent slips and eddies, I see the love of you

I stand forth to face the dawn to sally forth and carry on
The battle rages in silent sound the dance of victory to be found
The dragons careen about the skye watching each in golden eye
In times lost silvered room ringing sword and songs of now

I move in the silken night a victor home from this fight
The dragons carry the foes away to heal for the next fray
This my lady sees in now and holds me close strokes my brow
The daemon lust of battle gone now love and peace a gentle song

We walk upon the shores tonight memory of god's new light
Love is within the hearts so true the love of then the love of you
I wish to feel you close to me, stand and watch the teeming sea
Waves forever kiss the shore, my soul with yours wishes to soar

I dance in the golden light I sing the songs of the fight
My heart does cry for you today, my soul to wish you this day
When I see the changing day with dew and flowers on the quay
I move in memory to your side, with you and I and the changing tide

Poetry by Micheal Hopkins

Micheal Hopkins

Hell and Heaven

Stand tall shouts the soul, wind thrills
Marching in single row eyes down all save the one
Who dares mock the gates of time
What sort of creature are you

I am the warrior bowing to no man
Accepting no god, I am the warrior
Time smiles who is your master oh warrior
I have no master I am no one's slave

Time turns the clouds cease their travel
The wind stands in silent awe
Show me your soul warrior open wide
The warrior turns removing his sword

My soul is my steel, steel is my soul
Pure with singing edge this is my soul
Time laughs pure, pure is your soul
Look to your soul warrior look to your soul

See the stain see the blemish look to your soul
Remember and grieve you mocker of eternity
There upon the edge you so proudly flaunt
The stain, of loves lost tear

Look upon my face look upon the mirror
Look to your heart here is your mistress
Emerald eyes of fire and power
Emerald eyes of loves grace

Upon the mirror and upon times face
Deep within the warriors' heart
Emerald eyes and the remembrance of you
Pain of lose pain of sorrow pain of shame

Continued...

Yes, warrior remember the face emerald eyes
Now to the line and take your place
To the gates of hell, you are being borne
You betrayed her half a millennium before

You betrayed her and pay the penance forever more
Moving in silent single file to hells portal
And time did smile, for the end of another race
Dissension wiped from eternity's face

Deep within the heart of desire
Deep within times taunts fuel the fire
Upon the stain steel soul, I see the image of you
Looking back at me, emerald eyes fuel my fire

With shout of love regained with shout of defiance
Time looks seeing the steels tainted edge begin to heal
I am the warrior and time is my slave
Damn your hell for heaven I crave

Steel flashing in dragon's eyes
Time moves on and ignores the prize
Heaven's gate is open wide
For love is the key to get inside

And with warriors cry and battle oath
I love you more than life itself
The warrior enters upon the plain
Heaven's gate is shut again

But for the now the warrior will smile
His heart will sing and soul is pure
Steel and loves lost tear, And visions of you

Final Battle

And in the quiet time of lost and battered hope
The warrior in his silent tread ascends the final slope
And in the times of wistful hope and dreams of yet to be
He stands upon the edge of nothing and looks at eternity's sea

I call upon the gods above to see the pain that I feel
To show me hope and strength and love
But only emptiness I feel
And in the lost and darkened now and all the befores again

I move to join the battle in the abyss
To live and fight again, he begs her for the key to all
The end of agony but silence is the gift she gives
No gentle words spoke she

I move and face the endless foe in battles times before
And now the end of my quest is at eternity's door
I promised to be the best and faithful to the end
And now in hopeless sorrow into battle I descend

Upon the field of dragon's night and soulless hells I stand
The future once a flowering garden now trampled in the sand
I fought and waited in silent honour for what I cannot say
For knowledge of your love I sought but never would you say

Now onto the fields of trampled and twisted dreams
Upon the grass of loves sweet caress
Upon the stones of heartfelt pain
The final battle of my soul

The fight of dragons does remain
And while I stand and hold steel high the promise I do keep
The price of steel and of love both blood and oh so steep
I move upon and seek my foe a dragon of dark light

Continued...

The emerald eyes of holy fire does light my star cursed night
I know the words and hear the sounds but nothing is to me
For I have chosen the field to set my heart
To slay my dragons, you see

Now you are with the one you wish and I am not that one
So as my night is coming fast and the sorrow kills the sun
I stand with steel held in place and shield I cast aside
For to challenge the dragons of my heart the battle is inside

I move towards the central place and kneel upon the ground
My armor I cast aside and my sword is upon the ground
I offer up my throat and smile to dragon's view
Talon is a quick clean cut and my last vision is of you

I cry my soul is racing free and silence in the night
I love you more than life itself my darling my Blue Skye

CHAPTER 2

Azure Waters

Azure Waters is a continuation of The Ancient Warrior poems. The poems in this book show more of The Ancient Warriors quest for love and acceptance of his fate. I hope you will enjoy these poems as much as I enjoyed writing them.

Azure Water

Across the azure water beneath the silken skye
The lady stands to see the dawn, I smile
The winds do move the times the sands upon her shore
The golden keys upon her breast the way of heaven's door

Oh, can the sounds of another day the laughter of the next
Can the times of forever rest so lightly on her breast
I move in the times of other worlds the stars and the moon
The diamonds upon gods black velvet, night upon the world

She takes the smile I offer her I offer the heart in my hand
The time she strolls, time she smiles, the dreams of parched land
Take the plains upon the rolling hill the rock upon the sandy sea
The trees on the barren plain the innocence of me

Would you smile to hear a dragon sing an imp dance the skye
Would you laugh to see a daemon wander eating lemon pie
Could the silly things of worldly light catch your attention still
Or are the clouds the stars the heavens the playground of your mind

Oh, lovely lady of my lake the mystress of my mind
A Smile I give to see you dance a wraith in other time

Could Be

Sounds in silence, laughter in tears, smiles in sorrow
The fate of man the joke of time, eternity rolls on
Dragons shake their diamond scales scattering dreams around
Daemons seek to gather flowers littered upon the ground

I move to seek the smiles of time, the wishing of a dream
Oceans crash upon the shore, washing souls away
Clouds scatter to form again, heavens light gently filters in
Once upon a dream in time, the wishes of the next

Could time and tide, man his soul, life but a gentle ride
Woman sees her place in worth man sees the thorn
Roses upon your sleeping brow, life's mantle gently worn
Laugh with me, chase a dream, cast tomorrow aside

Chasing life seeking a wish, to run on times sandy plain
The mountains stand forever but lose substance grain by grain
And all that we see all that we do does it matter naught
Or is life to live, tomorrow to dream, love to savor, Could Be

Could

The tattered, battered soul of times past, the doomed
But the one doomed to live, the life that is not through
Can the light of tomorrow shine in the darkness of now
Is the cold breath of hell, just the beginning of my end

Can the steps of my dragons crush the heart
Will the breath of my daemons move the clouds
Should the shores of time recede to open my way
Can an evil being bring good to the world but not himself

Should the ends of time be the beginning of hell
Will the eyes of the dragons cry emerald tears
Can the joys of a friend end the prison of self
Would you, could you, have you now

Am I trapped in the loop of eternity
Or just traveling the periphery of now
Will all be seen and could it be seen in the tear
Will my soul shine or smolder and be dust in god's eye

Micheal Hopkins

Dreams of the Heart

Will the world see me as the dreams of my heart
Or will the world move aside to kill it from the start
I wish and that is my armor, I need and that is my sword
The soul senses, sees, and hears the meaning of the words

Can the world let one have the dreams of the heart
Will the gods know and feel what we knew from the start
Would you care to back away to run from your need
I will stand and face the hopes and live my emerald dreams

The dragons march upon the plain the dust of tattered time
The daemons smile upon the clouds the fluff of wasted dream
I stand and watch you in the mist the shape of things to come
I wait, I smile, I know you will be the only one

You can feel the heart, can hear the soul, can see my truth
The only things that the gods do bring is the living proof
You are the one the only need that I have upon the earth
The one you wish is the one you need, I stand before you now

Fly High

Fly high upon the sand
Fly high upon the land
Set your soul free this day
Fly upon the skye

Move to the winds of love
The passion of the day
Walk in silent union with your heart today
Fly high upon your life, fly up away

See the times for what they are
Eternity one instant in time
Forever the beginning
The end never insight, fly high

Upon the crystal night, angels see
The dragon smiles
Gods watch in silent repose
Fly high, live the love, bless the soul

Seek upon the plains of time and space
Seek the peace, seek the love
Seek the dragons golden face
Seek the knowledge of the race

Fly high and seek the skye
Seek the times with me
Move my love in times embrace
Fly high my skye with me

Micheal Hopkins

Green Hell

Green Hell long tossed nights, sleep a wish
Movement to the fore, sounds in muffled mysts
Shapes glow in white phosphorus dance
Once again yet once more

Charlie the unwelcome visitor
Knocking on my bunkers door
Come in says I come to the light
Smoke and talk wile away this night

Come in says I come to the dance
Weapons drawn the battles last song
Hell in the morning daemons in the night
Green Hell for the youth of man, survivors in the night

Lonely Soul

Twice I laughed and thrice I cried to hear the devil wind
Only in the dancing singing songs never known
The dragon moves in silent step seeking yet another home
Enter friend and evil foe both are you to me

Step lightly move in graceful rhythm bind your soul to me
We are the same yet each is different still
Walking, laughing, crying, singing in eternities' sea
You find as I that time is not our savior or enemy

But trapped in time our eternity we may never see
Come join me now here in my castle made of sand
Ground fine with eternal tread these hopes and dreams
Lost forever to mere mortal man

Sally forth, to charge the foe, reflections of you and me
A dragon's roar, a warrior's cry, life death or victory
Lost in this merry dance upon this well-worn plain
The warrior finds his youth again bathed in dragon's flame

Memories

The dream fades but the pain remains, my dragons roar
I walk in the moment seeking the time that was but never again
My lady smiles from mysts of time, to move from my view
My mind echo with your song, the laughter of then

Daemons stand in silent tears crying in the wind seeking skye
Slowly the moving heavens turn to velvet black and stars I see
But what of diamonds in the skye when the heart feels no thrill
Tears move to course my cheeks burning etching my memory

Walking the fallow plain dreams shattered, realities harsh hand
Clouds seek to comfort me, of heavenly grandeur but loss
The warrior dons his armor the steel within his grasp
Stride forth to seek the foemen to revel in the past

Walk with me within my prison call to my soul, remembrance
I stand in silent sorrow, the dream fades still pain remains
Skye bring my dragons home, call my daemons to my side
The remembrance the pain the loss of love deep within, a tear
A smile a burning thought my wish to see forever to be naught

Misspent Youth

Soft flowers memory of times before yet again
Skye to shelter hearts from seeking wind, dreams
Travel upon times charging steed, tilting for mans need
Flowers upon plains in settled grace, gentle sun upon the face

Clouds to memory, dreams to the soul, ageless wonder
Stepping forth to see the gods, to chase idle moments, laughing
Dance the ladies sing the songs, imps to meld the days in joy
Running the fields, a butterfly the sight
Wandering through shadowed night

Child of man stands in silent regard; living is easy aging so hard
The spirit does harden the price wisdom demand the knowing
Laugher to pay the piper of time, what would the maker of rhyme
Come the dawning in shadows gray to bring the youth he must pay

Oh, child of time eternity's prince the need must be the proof
Years fled the marker of thine to pluck the fruit from your vine
The calling the charge the payment is due
Misspent youth the pay is you
Can in the times of now and in the past
Know my child youth will never last

Never More

Crashing oceans, screaming skye, devils smile
Angels in silent row form upon the wind, the times
The stars to wink a silent tear, to darken, to die
The heavens shudder in frenzied myth

The worlds turn but slow, to drift in the great abyss
Moons shine in day's last light, suns blossom in the dark
The daemons gather the clouds, for the final keep
Songs of lost innocence, songs of eternal sleep

The earth blazes in emerald green the skye azure
The dragons speak, to sing and dance, the end has begun
Warriors kneel, to seek the solace, ladies to seek the smile
The kingdoms seek another time, honour held on high

The poet moves to see the sun to see the golden light
The lovers see in gathering shadow the gift of eternal night
Times heart beats in steady pace, eternity stands by
Children wonder aloud, where stars go to die

The tempo speeds the time draws near the times of never more
The heavens thunder with the sound, waves on times distant shore
The Lady smiles to see the end the answer to the quest
The death of light and birth of dark

Tomorrow is another day

Perfect Time

Slowly turning in his silence, the warrior seeks the light
The shapes of shadows and the song of sirens the wishing
Waves crash in silence oceans dance upon the edge
The sands move to make the daytime shaping tomorrow

The warrior moves slowly forth the vision to seek today
The lady on the mountain and the daemons on the quay
Would the wind carry my soul today or will the rain cleanse it so
The times and tides of forever, gods they are moving oh so slow

Wishes in the golden night and dreams upon the sand
And in the closing hours when the sun does seek to flee
Would you hold my hand in yours and carry the song along
Then when the darkness falls our souls will join the song

Times shifting shadows and worlds that turn away
The only thing that matters is will the lady stay
And when the end of forever does kiss the shores of time
The lady and the warrior will find their perfect time

Prisons

Lost upon the rim lost within the dream
Times upon the edge of tomorrow this and nothing more
The sands seek to cover; the clouds seek to hide
The seas and shores of forever in the land where he abides

Could not the changing list and the can't of never be
Would the flowers of the garden be a wreath for eternity
The dragon moves in his silent gait, the daemon at his side
The warrior in the locks of time forever to reside

I see in the mysts the turning of my soul
The shapes and the sounds of life so long ago
The lady moves to kill the sight, to move the dreams away
The times of the now the prison of today

I run to the mountains I seek the distant shore
The raging fires of love and hurt upon the evermore
Could time be a healer or would eternity change the game
Prisons of the soul, lost love one in the same

Really

Wishing the turn to change, the chance, the sounds
Dreaming the best, fearing success, cheering a smile
Walking the difficult but finding the ease of distress
Stand upon the shore the wind to caress your face

The sun warms your smile the spray washes your soul
Time is the essence of your prison, hurry the stain of our soul
Would you crush the rose in passing but stoop to taste its nectar
Grasses tickle the underside of heaven, angels laugh

Clouds shade harshness stars bath tomorrow before the sun
Walking the smile, lanes of silent dreams glowing with honour
Waves wash the sands the scouring of times tarnish away
Move the heart, shake the soul, run upon the plain

He walks, she smiles, he laughs, she bows, they know
Take the need, to need to be the castles of our dreams
Over the hills under the trees peace seeks our time
Breezes sing upon the wind soft as a daemons sigh

Rose Kissed Cheek

Twisted shadows on tomorrow's plain, tears of gods in the wind
Running laughter and sheltered smiles, love in the morning
Shape my heart and kiss the dreams of my soul
The wonder, the time's seas to caress my burning face

Warrior's dream or daemon's curse, slipping of wonders sands
I wander to the sound of song, ancient in time's, silence
The eternal night but a moment in lover's eyes
Promises stand in golden light upon tomorrow's rim

Dances in time and dancers in step to sounds no one hears
Merrily spinning the wonders of today the wishes of the next
Run to the rivers of emerald tears to taste bittersweet happiness
Climb to caress the skye, to feel, to ride ships of clouds

The sun born, lives dies, the moon to mourn the sun's passing
The silvered light of darkness to give birth to tomorrow's gold
Dragon smiles reflected upon diamond scales to seek
Loves caress upon your rose kissed cheek

Sliding

Sliding forward careening off the walls of time
I stand to dust eternity from my clothes
What and of what purpose is life when the end is so near
To laugh does it last longer, to cry does it change any

No, the times are the same happy sad, long or short
Can you move the rocks of eternity, for what purpose
Can you measure infinity, could you care to see the tally
I move to the hill once again, to rush headlong to the wall

The edge stands, the wall forever, the abyss all-powerful
I move to challenge the times, to curse the gods, to laugh
The dragons look and approve daemons shudder
The gods turn to hide the smiles, I am the warrior

The walls do stand, the edge does stay, life goes on
The day turns to night the mares to moon and stars
The sun to die the heavens to bring forth diamonds to mourn
I stand upon the gates of hell and laugh, to live, to continue

Souls

He stands upon the souls of then, the wish of tomorrow
The times do move to cover soft dust upon the skin
Would the wish of his lost heart fall upon soft sand
Or should he find the lingering light, her soul upon his hand

The wild, the tame, the twisting ride he calls life in this time
The songs of faith, the drums of honour, the gentle sleep
I would wish to feel your healing heart you warm caress
The touch upon the cheek, the heart, my soul

Sands, winds, and clouds of cotton kind, I see
The shifting shadows of tomorrow the time we do not see
The moaning of a long-lost wind flowing across my dream
The soul, the heart, the gold of life I seek within your eyes

The tear the song the march of leaden feet
I could dance to dragon's tales or leap to daemon myth
But in the times of now and then the memory the dream
I see you stand upon the plain my soul held in your hand

Twilights Sleep

In twilight's sleep upon sweat stained sheets, the dreams begin again
Lightning flash and thunders roar it all begins anew
Green hell and stinking mud the heat melts your will
Stepping to the warrior's life gods I remember still

A flash of light, a roar of sound, my walls crumble down
Once again, the Abyss calls to me to live the life again
Would a dragon or a daemon pull me free from times shifting sand
Calling me pulling me down to the field again

Cries of pain, screams of hate, bravery the coward's savior
Why would one such as me ever return again
I cried, I laughed, I died in subtle forms
Again, the sounds, again the sights, again the game begins

Distant thunder lulls my mind the lightning fades away
Weary warrior and dragon's friend begin again
Building walls to hold back dreams keep the memories at bay
Gods let the sleep return and bring another day

Soundless songs, dances with no movement in sad tune
Only this will remain when the dreams come again
Souls entwined in pain and love
Remembering will never end

Dream and Wonder

I dream and wonder and wish true
That I may love and enter you
With gentle touch and guiding hand
I enter into your promised land

And in the heat and damp dark
I feel your love and see it spark
I move in you and you on me
Loves motion for now and eternity

I feel the moistness of your love
As your tightness fits like a glove
And deep inside where lovers glide
I leave my soul for you to hide

We moan we groan we cry out loud
We shiver and quiver for love avowed
And deep within your damp darkness do
I leave my soul far within you

We smile and laugh and serious to
I nuzzle and nestle and pull you to me
Loving laughing for eternity
And we dream the dreams of tonight

Angels Daemons and Gods

Walk quietly upon the night the masters are sleeping
Laugh softly in the darkness they have no clue to your seeking
One dance one kiss, the journey does remain yet to begin
Ancient warrior, dragons, man, the quest remains the same

Angels seek to console you and Daemons desire to control you
Gods care not what you seek nor what you do today
Silence moves upon times, face beyond eternities scream
So many pass before but leave no track upon the sand

Time washes eternity clean, polishing all away
Man builds his massive temples great halls and cities too
All to wear away from times slow rub
The sands to wash into the sea

What nature of creature dares to challenge time and nature
When the cards are stacked, the game is rigged what will you do
Daemons laugh at your petty efforts and Angels shed a tear
Gods look and wonder silent in their judgment

Do we win or do we lose or does it matter at all
The Daemons call the tune, the Angels preen their wings
The Gods take a notice for they care not if you win or lose
Only that you try, so build your dreams, challenge time, dance to
your song

Michael Hopkins

Shaky Sand

Shaky upon the sands, a smile, a look, a feel
The wish of all men, the desire of some, fear to others
The times, the waste, the greed, the need, the flower
I am but the one that sees in time, eternity a gentle shower

Could I but touch upon the reefs of your dreams
Could my thoughts touch the shoals of your soul
The winds of my passage to move your heart
The need of my smile to bring your laughter in return

The beach is littered with dreams, thoughts, needs
The islands of yesterday built on forgotten dreams of today
Dragons lounge in quiet splendor, the thought, the smile
Emeralds are but stones of coloured hue, worthless

Worth less than the instant of a tear, yet more precious
Precious than all the wants and could have beens in time
Would you see me but as the one who dreams
Could I touch you in the mind, a thought, a sound

The shores are littered with the losses of time
The eternal rocks but sand ground fine in passage
The heavens walk in the glow of the morrow
Your heart, your mind, your smile, the dream, without sorrow

Solstice

Times of smiles and times of tears, the earth wrapped in silent silk
Dragons walk on soft stepped feet gently kissing the ground
Daemons run to fall in laughter, giggling sprawls upon the snow
My lady walks in crystal glory, warmed by her inner glow.

The meeting of the times of now to change the day away,
The evening of the times to bring the spring anew,
Warriors move in burdened lines, frost upon the skyee
Foe men greet the day to languish in the sun

Shortest of the long-lost days, the times of eternity's changing
Love sees the heart of man, the lady sees his soul
Walk with me in crystal shards to cast diamonds to the skyee
And when the singing of the winds, makes dancing clouds on high

The next is coming on the run, the before does pass behind
The breath of rebirth heard on far, the horizon and the sun
Take our moment chase our dream, kiss the wintry skyee
Dragons seek the warming times, daemons dance in mirthful play

The warrior seeks the challenge the battle fully found
The lady seeks the heart of man to give love unbound
The skyee seeks the edge of time the clouds seek the night
 I seek the solace of you my love held so tight

CHAPTER 3

Crystal Shards

Crystal Shards is the continuation of the saga of the Ancient Warrior in his quest for love and peace. The visions of tomorrow and the memories of the past shape his actions of the present.

Crystal Shards of Forgotten Dreams

Crystal shards of forgotten dreams, melting in the sun
Times slow passage to wear away the edge of remembrance
Wishes of laughter, tears of joy, golden lovers on the rim
The edges of forever just a short walk this way, tomorrow

Dragons on the face of love, basking in the glow, slow dreams
Winds of change and winds of time the flavour of each day
The past is but a moment, the present gone to then
Future times rushing in
My lady dances in the mysts of times' shadowed reef, laughter

Daemons cry in sorrow, daemons cry in joy
Children comfort them today
Walking to the beat of souls singing in the light
Children lead them on
Following across the windblown skye, down upon the plain
Warriors cease to battle hell ceases its reign, peace

Winters blowing gales summers charging wind upon the world
Falling leaves kiss the earth and dance
Awaking worlds just within our grasp
The snow in the dance of souls, capering across the land
Lovers in quiet times strolling hand in hand, the peace of time

These are the way of things in the distant land
Smile my love take my hand
Walking in silent glen running along the shore, time stops for lovers
Eternity is a gentle memory, love rules the day, pain kept at bay
In the race of life each passing day, take the breath of freedom

In mundane and gray clad lands, the dragons sing no song
The daemons have no soul my love and eternity so long
The children fear the night the warrior fears the day
All seek to find the love, but mists pull it away

Continued...

Come to my world of light the world of golden dew
Where dragons sing of glory the daemons sing of you
The place in the now but of next and before, my world my dear
The castles on times gentle shore

Clouds of Tomorrow

Shining in silent smiles the world moves on
My heart in joyous song my dance that of ancients
Would the dragon cease to fly or daemon to laugh
For the kiss of a maiden's lips upon their mighty brow

Neither dragon nor daemon touch the clouds today
A warrior's heart in merry dance to caress the skye
Sands and time the eternal quest moves on
Chasing golden shadows across the face of love

I seek in the turning to see you yet again
The next or this now who will know
Before on the fields with battle hot and near
Joyful singing steel thrust of battle spear

Come my love to seek the edge kissing times hoary face
Silent memory of times long gone echo in this place
Run to see the clouds, ships of tomorrows dream
Chase our dreams of evermore, emeralds in your eyes

Micheal Hopkins

Clouds

To stand, to see, to hear the wind
I feel the clouds pull at my feet, the skye's cry for me
I am the wind dancer, the one, free
I move and play upon the skye the clouds and the sea

I chase the clouds about the raging skye
The moon is my plaything the gods my mates
I run the ridge and climb the mountains
Tempting, laughing, ignoring the fates

Up to the stars and into the sea
The froth, the foam, the sand, the time
I am the wind dancer and chase the skye
The dancer the singer of time

Crystal Spires

Love's tears crashing onto time's cold face
Changing, turning, and falling in place
Warmth blazes on heart's desire
Faces of love reflection in crystal spire

Wheeling turning ever changing
Dreams walk upon eternity's soulless face
Mirrors with no reflection, voices of love
Caring, sharing, and blessed from above

Demon night patrols this place
Home of hope on god's great face
Moving in silent rows stand thoughts
Dreams of long ago

Your face on shattered tears
Your voice echoes in long deaf ears
Smiles change and heavens die
Only souls will possess the skye

Moving ever in one place
Rushing quietly to slow the pace
Turning, watching, seeing with blind eyes
Long lost visions of paradise

Loves tears crashing onto times cold face
Building Crystal Spires
On eternity's face
Longing and loving desire of you

Counting eternity, the numbers too few
Wishing, crying to build the spire
Hearts burning with loves cleansing fire
While loves tears crashing onto times cold face

Crystal Days

Mornings upon the mystic haze smiles in the shadows
Dragons move to seek the light to dream of the skye
Mornings of the crystal day, diamonds placed in time
Moving forward to the next, the tears of love a gentle reign

Sands move in silent dance to see eternity's shore
Waves of time wash the souls healing warmth gentle kisses
Man comes to the day a wonder in its gift
The lady dances to seek the dawn holding golden light

Crystal Days upon the face to bless the mortal man
Daemons sing of times before of this and other lands
Drifting upon a sea of time the world carries on
The wish of time is for the passing the wish of man everlasting

River's flow towards the edge cast upon the shore
Shadows crept from the night to chase the sun away
But silver moon with diamond stars do promise another day
Kiss the breeze caressing your face the wind to sing you through

A crystal day so clear to ring the songs of hearts this way
The dance of innocents the rhymes of desire
The emerald promise in times great vault
A wish this day to never end, the times to keep at bay

Crystal Dress

Upon the winds and sands, she stands to see the tide
The lady in the crystal gown, the goddess, the dream
The dragon bows in quiet praise, to weep, to smile
The daemon walks the edge of then the now

The heavens open in emerald glory to fall upon the land
The gods cast the die again, taking fate by the hand
The game goes upon the skye the players in a row
The lady in the crystal gown walks upon the sea

The times roll in frenzied froth, jewels glisten in the sun
The lady gathers in the sight, to sigh, to smile, to laugh
The treasures of the world she holds within her heart
The lady seeks to comfort man to embrace the coming night

Dance

And he smiles she laughs
The stars shine and she smirks
He shakes it she takes it
The world turns and it is done

But he says yet again she smiles
And glides on in
He smiles she smirks he twitches
She jerks, he moans she groans

The world turns and time passes
He rolls to the right she to the left
He says well is it right
She says darling just right

She says is it tight
He says it's wonderful
She smiles he smirks
The world turns time passes

He runs she follows
He turns she shies
He loves she sighs
He wants she needs

He takes her hand
She takes his heart
She smiles
She loves he needs

His to Stay

When in the walking times the runners come to rest
The lovers on the shores of time seek the peaceful best
Could you in the morning and would you in the night seek a kiss
The shapes and mysts of evermore our castle in the mists

Dragons dance and laugh their regal way, smiles and happiness
The daemons run to seek your smile to brighten up the day
The sun shines to warm your cheek, the moon to warm your heart
The souls of our eternity the velvet softness of the dark

Time slows for us today to give each minute the wish
Ah the scent of roses in the wind and the taste of your kiss
Walking hand in hand today upon the sandy shores
The wishes of the eternals, the forever mores, our time

The winds do blow to caress your smile to warm your cheek
The warrior in his armor bright, you the one he seeks
Would you in the coming times kiss his tears away, for he knows
That in the future and in the past that you are his to stay

Micheal Hopkins

Eternity and Beyond

I see the edges of frayed promise
The tattered fringes of lost desire
All this in the wasteland of yesterday
The dust of times lost winds blows in silence

If eternity were a kingdom would time be the prince
And the warrior would he too have a place
I walk the shattered path of peace and tranquility
Having once treaded the broad avenues of battle

Honour and duty are my armor
Desire and need are the fuel of my warrior's heart
Love of you the standard under which I serve
Your name the cry of battle and glory

In the distance, I see the dragons of the heart
Row upon diamond scaled row, standing silent
Muted by loves lost tear, chained in the now
I am the warrior and the dragons my foe

And upon the field of stagnant tears
Rimmed by the dusty road of forgotten dreams
I stand and draw my steel and cry forth your name
Blue Skye, for honour, for duty, for love, for you

Dragons' chains released eyes upon the warrior
Answer the cry they do, Eternity and pain are for you
Steel against the skye and I sally forth
Blue Skye, for honour, for duty, for love, for you

Battle joined warriors cry and dragons roar
Steel sparking on diamond scales glistening in golden blood
Tooth and talon rending and tearing crimson spray
The warrior thrusts and parry, lean and dodge

Continued...

The tear the treasure the key to long lost dreams
The release the freedom of shackled love
I strike and shout your name
The dragon roars with eternity's pain

Forward into the fray living or dying this day
I will win the tear and free the dreams
Or will die to live no more on eternity's timeless shore
Blue Skye, for honour, for duty, for love, for you

The plain is silent, washed in crimson and golden gore
The victor alone and bloodied on times endless shore
Eternity's pain and times silent prison stand open
The end of all or the beginning again

The warrior bends and sees the emerald eye
The eye so clear and so true and the tear
The tear the freedom the key to dreams and you
Take the tear and hold it tight
Blue Skye, for honour, for duty, for love, for you

Micheal Hopkins

Involved Not

Sit quietly on the sidelines, involved not
Watch the world see the Skye, involved not
Cry to the gods, smile in the night
Walk the trails of forever, behind

The fear, the sorrow, the haste, to leave love behind
Walk to the shore see the froth
Dragons in the heavens, Daemons in the mind
Sit quietly, involved not

I challenge the heart, you parry the quest
I am the warrior, you the lady, come to me
Involved not you cry, dragons weep, gods sigh
I wish you, I need you to try

Involved not in life, for love is so rare
The emerald tear, the wind in the air
I wish you; I want you, to know
Involved for that is loves gentle glow

Morning Upon

Morning upon the sands morning upon the sun
Morning upon the shores the crests the shoals
Morning upon the skye the clouds the heavens
Morning upon the sun the dark upon the moon

Morning upon the snowcapped range, the ridge
Morning upon the plains upon the verdant green
Morning upon the sands of time tinted in emerald sheen

Morning upon the winds the daemons silken skin
Morning upon the dragons the fur upon their chin
Morning upon the stars the diamonds of the night
Morning upon your lovely face, gods a beautiful sight

Sweet Sweet Wine

Laughter in the silence the sounds of lover's sighs
The shapes and times of tomorrow, seen in my lady's eyes
The drum, the beat, the songs of heart, the moving hand of time
Wishes in the silence the dreams to come anew

Wandering your innocence and marvel at the sights
The stars of a million years the moons of velvet nights
Shadows cast in loves long quest and questions in the day
When in the times of now can the hints of loves smile abide

My dragons are searching the perfect rose to find
The daemons set the tables and pour the finest wines
Winds scented with orchids, and flowers scented with you
The meal of the after the present the new

When in the seas of time, the gods do seek the seal
That which is holding hearts in golden bond, the souls set free
And when in the course and when the rivers cease to wind
The knowing of your love for me, the finest sweet sweet wine

Twice Upon the Dream

Stand fast my silent friend the future is drawing near
I seek to see where I go wondering where I have been
But truth be known the joy of dreams fill my empty thought
Fragile are the hopes of man seeking the answer why

But in blindness seeking with eyes upon the ground
Silvered shards of shattered dreams diamonds on the sand
While silent, waiting, seeking tomorrow, a song
But tomorrow is shaped not by dreams but the gods' gentle hand

Time moves upon eternity's sea, sand washed from your soul
Are we who we seek to be or yet another's dream
If in the waking will we be but shadows until his return
Am I just within your sleep a horror or pleasant breath

Laughter found in silent song daemons dancing in the wind
Another dragon held within seeking freedom still
Or can we find that we are but the shards of dreams
Resting bright and silent upon the sand

Walk

Walk twisting turning, only to view anew tomorrow
Dancing to the sounds of dragon song, laughter in the moment
I stand loudly silent upon times ship, crossing eternity
Far shores kissed by the winds, near shoals shadowed by the abyss

Sing songs of ancient times, tempt the gods, warriors of forever
Move in silent step, heavens heart beat an eternity
Could man dream a dragon dream or dance the daemon heart
Time only in silent tread to mark life sands but for the instant

She sings her song, cast upon emerald waves, to haunt, to call
How does man resist her call, her soul calling for you
Run in eager search, the hunt but another game, to find to hold
I hear the songs of sirens, the dance of dragon pure, daemon laughter
upon the wind

Hold close your soul washed in emerald tear, cleansed in eternal fire
Give your heart of burnished gold freely upon times alter a gift
Sing your songs of life and loss of times of never been
But hold your love close a smile upon your soul

Golden Mane

Upon the rolling plain she rides smiles in the sun
Wind does caress the clouds in gentle row
She rides upon the golden beast the earth passing by
The horse of golden mane flowing in the sun, to ride

The passing moment, the time of bridled joy
The need to be saddled, to earth, skye, and wind
The lady astride the gentle beast, to run a raging skye
Golden manes flags upon the winds

Micheal Hopkins

I Will Keep the Smile

When in the times of tomorrow the world shades its smile
The warrior cries a single tear the dragon stops a while
The turning of tomorrow, the look of today, clouds in flight
The moon in silver mantle the velvet of the night

The lady walks upon the hill the warrior upon the plain
The seas see all as nothing but sand, to come again
I move in the distant sounds of laughter in your soul
My heart climbs the battlement the walls steep but soft

The daemon enters the dance to bring the sun around
And gods in their heavens do call this hallowed ground
Would in the course of time eternity change his smile
The world in a dance of light the fragrance in the mind

Flowers on the mountain and ships of clouds in the air
The scent of dew and nectar, the softness of her hair
The warrior cries a single tear the dragons stop a while
But time in remembrance and for you I will keep the smile

Smiles Upon the Plain

Turning in the times of now, the next, to see the shadows
Wishing for the smiles of others to lighten the burden of now
Winds whisper secrets only hearts will hear, laughter on the plain
Clouds in regal row, sail the azure skye, storm whipped smiles

Running in unison, steps out of time, eternity forgiven
Ladies of luster shining in silent humour to see the satin soul
Warriors dancing seeking, to tire the daemons joy of abandon
Dragons tiptoe into heaven to watch the merry sight

Stars cry diamonds, the moon bleeding silver light, velvet night
Children laugh ladies smile warriors blush caught in dance
The daemon plays the fiddler's song gods call the tune
Smiles upon the plains of life love in the light of the moon

Companion souls to share the time's laughter in your smile
Life the game, a sadness thing but seek happiness for the while
Angels in heaven's gate do smile when you laugh the skye
Happiness a fragile thing exercised or will die

Soft Rocks

The rocks do seem so soft today, the clouds so hard
The gold is a burnished red, the emeralds polished and old
The seas gently lap on eternity to wash times to the world below
I walk in the silent memory of what was and is and will be again

The lady stands in shrouded mist a mystery a dream a wish
The wind reveals but hides to show yet another view
The skye is darkening light, the silence golden
The heavens move to strike the earth to shake loves foundation

Times and troubles tides and tribulations mean nothing, here
Trees kiss the earth and skye, leaves sing to wind passing by
Could the well of souls the dream of the heart produce, will it be
The rivers of time wash the beach the shore the rocks of me

Take the measure give the fill; charge the dragons upon the hill
Daemons to seek the way the treat the path of lightness
The feet move to silently stand dancing stepping upon the hand
The mysts the lady the times the winds, worth the life let it begin

The Fisherman

Upon the shores, the lakes, the rivers of time, she stands
Casting forth to seek her prey, the wish, the need of now
The line, the hook, the weight, holding dreams on the sand
Could the lady move to now, the fore, the time, the sand

I see her in the fading light, the stars of heavens pride
The smiles in her heart, the joy, the soul, the beauty inside
Cast forth the lure, the seeking, the dreams soft mouth
Clouds and winds racing souls upon heavens shine

She sends the thoughts, the hopes, and the fears
Waves and motions in time, the catch a triumph
Feel the tug, the pull, the need, the taking of the gift
The offer to the souls of time, the eternity, the wall

Micheal Hopkins

Tomorrow's Wishes

Dreams are but the shapes of tomorrows wishes
Words are but the movement of the air, softly falling
Why so the cut the wound the sharp edge of such gentle things
The cutting edge of words in anger, words in pain

Wishes only bring smiles, dreams but the promise of hope
Words shatter the dream, poison the wish, making tomorrow gray
Darkness encompasses the dreamer, a wish sour upon the heart
I look but see nothing no joy only the darkness of forever

Tomorrow the emerald gem of desire now flawed and fractured
What oh gods can destroy my wish, darken my dreams
Words, spoken in anger cried in anguish sour upon the soul
Hope, a wish a desire but nothing shines in the night only darkness

The lady, the warrior dragons dance in glee for freedom they seek
The rending the pain as my dragons burst free from my soul
To wreck havoc upon the plains of dreams, yet again
The lady stands in sadness as she frees her dragons too

Daemons frolic on the edge of tomorrow, tossing dreams aside
Movement, but not towards the smiles which would grow
Sadness in silence a tear burning my cheek, to etch my scarred soul
The jewel now just fragments in the sand, promise forgotten

Foe men stand in rank and row to watch the dragons tear
The sounds of battle silent yet in mortal combat we begin
One will leave the plain a victor, the other vanquished to the shadows
What price victory, is tomorrow worth the cost if the now must
perish.

Continued...

Thrust and parry, challenges met and given, dragons dance in glee
The battle of him and her
Victory is but an illusion for what is the cost to win
Can the times of forever can these live again, Questions
I move to parry you thrust to win the battle rages on

Words soft and gentle things, cutting souls in twain
The burning of your dragons' fire, the furrow of your talon
My soul burns in torment, my mind cries for peace
But a warrior has his life to live, his dreams of evermore

The lady seeks a solace the warrior seeks a peace
The dragons seek the blood of souls devoured piece by piece
The gods move to distant sides to view the battle fierce
And in your call for silence the warrior's soul you pierced

Wishes In the Snow

Sparkling laughter glistens upon the land
Diamonds in white, times eternal sand
Take this moment hold this dream
Run in the sunlight chasing shadows

Roses kissed in the night dew in the holding
Dragons dance to the sounds of nothing
Daemons dream of tomorrows smile
Wishes in the snow, heaven on the rim

I wander in the glory of you, love forever now
Kisses on your eyes smiles in your heart
Love me for the time love me in the night
Hold me close upon your dreams eternity beyond

Shards of past pain, lie shattered in the mysts
Step in the light of time, my lady dragon kissed
I love you in the moment I love you in the all
Love to my Shy Lady, till all the stars do fall

Goodnight by Carol Hopkins

CHAPTER 4

Sands of Time

Sands of Time is a collection of Ancient Warrior poems expressing his love for the lady. Some of the writings are a little risqué while others express his deep need and feel for the love he seeks. His quest for the one and only love in his life.

August Nights

We enter the gloom some call a room
At the top at the head of the stair
In the quiet and in the dark and in the cool August air
I was so young and inexperienced too

The lady was a dream a vision a god's delight
The lady was here with me this cool august night
I came close she did too, the passion the love the need too
I remember hot sex on cool august nights

We slowly learned as she taught the art to me
The art the soul the time the need to set it free
I felt the breath the taste the sound
The mood the love the scent the ground

Cool August nights the dream of my youth
The loving the joy the living the proof
I love you she said I mouthed a reply
She cried a tear, I never knew why

We joined and we coupled and sweated a bath
We were in such a heat of passion we bettered by half
In the darkness and in the light the passion the love
On that cool August night

Micheal Hopkins

Fires Burning Bright

Words are wonders and you are my dream
Forming times and waves upon the sea
I move in the wonder of yesterday
Loving you is all to me nothing else exists

Three words just three words will hold
Yes the words will hold back the abyss
Three words only three from you to me
And the future will shine

If the words are not to be found
I am on the slipping ground, a tear
Burning in my vision but darling
You have made the final decision

So free me from the promise of destiny unbound
Free me from the quaking slipping ground
For I will seek the fire and the dragons smile
Eternity is my curse and love is the fee

For only in the loving can the soul be unshackled
With vision burned in tears fear of these remaining years
Walking and seeking time
My soul adrift on seas of sorrow

No longer the dreamer for my vision true
I only dreamed and dreamt for you
Now is painful memory I reside
Seeking the passion of the dragon inside

Drawing my sword and charging the gate
Crying for the battle before the stares of hate
Charging forth and through upon the sea of blue
Burning arching refusing to go down

Continued

And at the edge of eternity's abyss
My cry of battle is this and only this
On to the ramparts onto the walls
I love you more than life and now the curtain falls

Upon the plain of tomorrow rimmed by loves lost sorrow
The dragons await and with this cry I seek my fate
I love you more than life and now the curtain falls
Steel strikes diamond scales

And dragon cries resound from the walls
Parry and thrust guard again
Talons rake and tear the skin
Steel bites and draws cold blood

In a strike lightning, fast the dragon scores
I am done at last, cold blue fire does my soul cleanse
Broken and spent upon eternity's floor I cry to you
I love you more than life and now the curtain falls

My blue skye I see across times walls
The dragon turns his emerald eye and a tear
Bitter sweet against the gold
Crying for three words untold

Blowing in the Wind

The winds of time move in rhythm of the day, a smile
Waves gently wash the shores of time, to soothe the warrior's way
Shapes and forms of yesterday drift in the winding path
My love shapes the mind of man the wish of coming dew

Walk the gentle breath of love feel the warmth of you
My dragon smiles in silent peace my daemon sings the tune
Clouds do come and rain does fall in gentle heavens drum
The wish in smiles the wish in love the warming in the wind

Laughter in the silent room love upon the rim, joy
I move to the rhythm of my loves quiet touch the dream
Sands do move to build eternity for the mans own time
The would the could the taste of love the motions of the sea

Canyons in the mind of my lady mountains of the warrior
Slowly in the mood of love quickly in the dream, an eternity
I can and do she would and does he melts in her sighs
Dreams and wish and smiles in my lady's emerald eye

Autumn Smiles

A dream in time kisses upon the rose
Smiles on windswept plains, laughter dancing
Love upon the skye chasing clouds in azure fields
Warriors move in solemn dance to welcome tomorrow

Come laugh in my shadows race in my sunlight
Share times of forever love in velvet night
Wander dreams choose the wish of your desire
Join my dragons dancing in cold emerald fire

Time is but the maker eternity is but the dream
Forever but a moment in lover's eyes
Pluck your flowers weave our fairy crown
Race in times seas casting eternity's sands around

Tomorrow a wish today but yesterdays dream
My love a song of ancient times dressed in emerald green
I see you in my shadows dancing in pools of life
I hold you in my heart and soul forever

He Saw Her in The Distance

He saw her in the distance
He saw her in the sun, the moon the stars
He wished to know the lady
But he saw her from afar

Walking to the edge and fearful to enter in
He saw her in the distance the smile to invite
He saw that she was edging to the time of night
To enter in the darkness to stand upon the sand

He saw her in the distance he saw her in the sun
The light so dark it was sullen and he saw her beckon him
Into the dark and into the light into the life
He chose to see the other side, the love of now

He saw her in the mirror close upon his hand
He saw her with him walking upon the emerald sand
She smiled and the heavens cried the dragons roared
The sea did cease to froth, the lady he adored

They moved in the waves the currents of time
He flowed about her happily life a heady wine
He saw her in the mirror close upon his hand
He saw the world a happy place safe upon the land

Love My Lady Best

Should in the setting sun the tear of god be seen
For the night does blanket the softness of the emerald green
The seas do calm the wind does cease to kiss upon the land
The moon in its silver gown is coming close at hand

The warriors move from the field to rest the night away
The daemons seek to curl up to sleep from their play
The dragons mount the mountaintop
The children seek the beds

The lover's wake to see the night lands for them alone
They wander to the shores to watch the light to play
The stars kiss the heavens crying for the day
The lady holds her warrior close against the coming night

The times of dreams and mares which hold the weak in fright
The sleeping world does rest but in the darkness now others
The moving of the huntress the flight of the prey
But in all the times before and in tomorrow too

The coming of the morning light
The kiss of fragile dew
The flowers open wide to seek the suns caress
But of all these times and things I love my lady best

Loves Eyes

Walking and talking and smiling at tomorrow
Moving so slowly so deeply in memory of you
Half hidden remembrances and long buried desires
Laughter ringing in dark chasms of my mind

We ran, we laughed and darted among the shoals
Star-crossed lover's minds free, drinking the nectar of we
The one, the other moving, in shadows upon the wind
Dancing and chasing clouds across a raging skye

Gods smiled passing us by watching our flight to the rim
Stars were diamonds upon your hair the moon your smile
Cold but with deep moving within your soul
Loving and laughter the rhythm of the night

What in heaven or earth could still our delight
Cold smiles empty tears words fringed in fears
We loved yet was it enough, we laughed but tears burned our cheeks
Each seeking what private dreams lovers could seek

We raced and danced the wind, chased the clouds
I turned and you were standing so still
Your eyes glacial cold upon the hill
The fires are spent and love is not upon the stars

Life will not admit that love is enough
I cried, you looked upon my face the moons smile
Growing cold upon your face
I died in that moment of time

We parted you to yours and me to mine
Personal hells with torments of our own desires
An eternity stoking and feeding loves lost fires
Death of the soul dusting of the heart
Continued...

I walk the sands of remembrance and time
Dreaming of lost love in long lost time
Foot falls and muttered smiles
Light within the face of the smiling gods

Wind sings and clouds roar against the skye
Strange shadows are seen passing by
Wings of dusty memory past come to me
Healed at last I race the wind upon the sea

Micheal Hopkins

Loves Taste

Love upon his lips, the salty sweetness
The smell upon his being, the moistness
The slickness of his soul
And she is gone but a minute

While he lays and tastes her upon his being
He teases his mind with wonder
The pleasure of his seeing
Opalescent and glowing the loving of her now

Drying and sticking but still delicious
Yes delicious even now,
The sweet scent of her the taste upon the tongue
His fingers sticky but let me lick them still

For in the tasting and the memory
He will be drinking up his fill
Once more to feel her thighs upon his cheek
To see the satin hair and the curve of her face

And in the being to taste and fill within
The cumming of her love
The covering of his chin
The smile deep inside when his tongue did find

The sweetness of her being
So very deep inside
And when she felt him tasting her so deep
The grinding of her love and the silk upon his cheek

And now that the time is over
And she has gone away
The taste and smell will keep him, For yet another day

Never Stray

Slowing in times seas the future comes to pass, a dream
The shaping of tomorrow, gentle kiss of times sands at her feet
The waves to wash trouble from her mind and heart today
The dancing of playful dragons the children of the day

When in the sounds of song ancient and full of time
The lady walks upon the sands the world does in green shine
The flowers on the plains the aspens on the hill
The butterflies in gentle flight these excite my lady still

The castles in the shapes of clouds great halls of misty lore
The gentle laughter of the lovers upon this distant shore
Would you dance the times of evermore
Would you sing the songs of then
I wish in my silence to hold you once again

Running in the rivulets and walking in the sea
The charming times of now forever the love of you and I
I miss the laughter in the night and flowers in the day
But the warrior is coming home so soon to live to never stray

Micheal Hopkins

Night of Love

He stands at the foot of the table
She looks up to smile, to laugh to see
He knows she sees the blood but the eyes
The eyes see the times of peace

Standing and stretching she takes her silken scarf
To wipe the signs of battle from his ancient face
The eyes are merry the souls are light she is happy
The warrior bends to assist the lady her chore

She laughs hugs and kisses his wounds
The dragon to her side smiles with ivory mirth
The daemon on his left laughs and bows
She curtsies the gift she accepts the warrior smiles

She stands to say the times are now the wish is hers
She walks the narrow edge of wish and desires the edge
The blackness of nothing the light of it all
She grasps the stars by the glow to give his eyes

He sees the moon and the blush of slivery light
The skye the clouds hurry against the night
He bends to hold to carry to care
This night is for love comes let us prepare

Pace

Pace off the hundred
Pace off the thousand
Count the souls and feed the fire
Life and love and honour on the pyre

Move the dial change the hands
See it change see it stay the same
Run to the ridge wander the valley
Lay in the grass feel the flow of time

I will and you see I can and we should
The times the life the love the smile
Only in tomorrow can we see today
And only in today is yesterday so true

I wish you seek your thrill I cry
We are the now the time that is not before
Was the earth our soul would it be as large
If the heavens sought the sea would you laugh

When the moon walks the velvet skye
When the stars pierce the darkness full
When the heart screams in joyful song
Will we still love in the innocence of now

Micheal Hopkins

Passions Smiles

Times and seasons winds and tides the turning of life
We walk upon an emerald shore to seek a distant land
The wish of now is ever more the needs are in the fore
I turn to see the lovely face the face of loves beckoning door

The dragons sow and reap the harvest of smiles in the night
Daemons look to see the sounds love a beautiful sight
I stand with you in quiet shadow a kiss upon your eyes
Emerald tears upon the grass to grow love to giant size

We move in loves silent dance a smile upon your face
The eyes show a burning need a golden light upon your soul
I kiss the tears the salty dew and wish to hold you tight
Passions smiles abound in the beauty of our night

Plains of Ever More

Seven times in heaven thrice times in hell, love
The changing shapes of shadowed time the ringing of the bell
I move in the moment I run upon the plain
The wistful dreams of forever more once and once again

The rolling waves in times lost seas, the sands of change
The endless roar of eternity racing from the abyss
Clouds do sing in silent joy to race the skye this day
Wandering laughter dancing joy for you are here to stay

Lustful smiles and shy quick glance warm upon my skin
The dragons hold to the other the daemons join the din
Could in this moment, cold upon my soul I forget
Nay the thoughts of you are ever formed held within my heart

Seven times in heaven thrice times in hell, salvation
The seeking of your presence the comfort of your smile
Emerald eyes of passion the warrior falls within, to live
Upon the plains of evermore the life the love the you begin

Micheal Hopkins

Quest the End

Walk softly for the sand conceals the tracks of time
The oceans wash the memories of many before, the next
Winds drive the prints from the shore the cleansing
The warrior moves in silent tread to see but look again

I would but should that which I do be of me or the other
The wish of marching hoards to conquer the world, weak
The dreams of lusting man to capture the soul of beauty, false
The wishes of dragons for warm friends, cold fires, wonder

I would and you did, the dragon stands aside, the pride
The daemon in the step the shadow in the mind, the wildness
I charge to the fore but for what purpose, the need
The last is but the beginning the middle but the deed

I can will I who will say who will care the thought
Lady of the times and tide woman of desire
The fires of want and need, your presence build but higher
The warrior in the times of now the fires and the smiles
The love the touch the dream of you the quest, the end

Really

Wishing the turn to change the chance the sounds
Dreaming the best fearing success cheering a smile
Walking the difficult but finding the ease of distress
Stand upon the shore the wind to caress your face

The sun warms your smile the spray washes your soul
Time is the essence of your prison; hurry the stain of our soul
Would you crush the rose in passing but stoop to taste its nectar
Grasses tickle the underside of heaven, angels laugh

Clouds shade harshness stars bath tomorrow before the sun
Walking the smile lanes of silent dreams glowing with honour
Waves wash the sands the scouring of times tarnish away
Move the heart shake the soul run upon the plain

He walks she smiles he laughs she bows, they know
Take the need to need to be the castles of our dreams
Over the hills under the trees peace seeks our time
Breezes sing upon the wind soft as a daemon's sigh

Micheal Hopkins

Shadows of the Night

Shapes and times shadows in the night
Lovers on the shore the moon within their sight
The winds of tomorrow kiss their face now
The wonder of the moment the dream of the how

Walking in the silence of love upon the sand
The shadows of the next upon the silent land
Would you hold me close my love
To dance in eternal song, life the joy the wonder

The times so very long, a wish I hold within
The need to see you smile a kiss a laugh
The changing moods the long eternal mile
The taking and the giving the sharing of the heart

The souls of love entwined the moment just the start
The wonder of your touch the warmth of your skin
The tracing of your laughter now the love begins
The dragon laughs the daemon cries

Lovers in the night
Hope and the promise
The song of just right
A sigh

Shed the Frown

She sees the look he sees the laughter
She moves to the edge of tomorrow to laugh again
She sees forever in the instant promise of tomorrow in now
Could she feel the motion the ripples in the fabric

He sees her look he hears her question he listens to the now
The winds are there to change the day the clouds to dance
The wisdom she seeks is all around to pluck from the air
The need to see the times of then seem to her but fair

She walks the paths of distant time the shores of when to where
The lakes the streams the rivers of time the dance
She sees him she laughs; she hears him she smiles
He sees the edge of each abyss and the darkness glows within

She jumps the chasm to laugh to run to sing
The soul unsung the heart unfettered the dragons on the run
I should she would I can she will but does it matter now
For to see the smile she must shed the frown and unfurl the brow

Micheal Hopkins

She is Gone

Turn quickly too late she is gone
Rush in place the corner to find she is gone
Climb the wall storm the hill; seek her in the distance
She is gone, life the battle love the campaign

Move the arches move the pain
Climb the crest to see her again
Where oh turn so quickly she is gone
Off to the gate beyond the moats of time

Seek and quest the desire to make her mine
Travel the road taken by few, rocks the tread
Love your desire the path upward into the pit
Love the quest the compass of passion

Seek and turn quickly again, she is gone
Look to the gods the heavens are closed
Mind the music rush the walls look to your self
Look to your soul she smiles and beckons you in

Slanting Trees

Windy skye clouds rushing the sun, earth dances
Walking upon grasses tickling gods feet, a kiss
Moons stand upon the realm wisps of tomorrow, shadow today
Sands drift to seek the level the fill a leveling

Would you smile to see dragons dressed in clouds
Daemons shower in mist angels dance upon the sea
The sounds of tomorrow twist in a rhyme, wondering
Taste today the wind brushes the trees the leaves

I seek to see a new day, a freshness of the morrow
Taste the smile of happiness the nectar of love
Could you run to laugh to see the next or stand to be the now
A question a wish a dream a wonder, the next or now, but never
before

Micheal Hopkins

Smiles and Tears

Walk in the fore the vanguard to see the day
I see upon the horizon clouds the sentinels of tomorrow
The skye upon the land in gentle glory
The wind to brush your face to caress to soothe

I am the warrior the one standing alone
The tear you see but a memory of my dream
Dreams move in regal rank sparkling in heavens light
Smiles stand upon the shore tempting times wrath

I see you upon the mists the plains of desire
Silent monument to loves lost tear shining
The smile you offer sad but so bittersweet needing
The dream a cry for today a promise of tomorrow

The warrior walks his lonely fate the tear upon his cheek
Loves diamond shining in the sun
The smile his promise of remembrance the wish
The warrior seeks the mist the you the promise of the fire

Winters Wish

When time and smiles kiss the crystal frost, I dream
On shores wreathed in dreams of forever, I smile
The wash the winds the crashing waves, a promise
My love my life today tomorrow forevermore

Walking with my lady, dancing in golden sun
Spirits of the next angels in the snow
Come my dream my darling my winters goddess a kiss
To hold to have to keep safe forever in the warmth of my soul

I seek to hear your laughter I pray to see your smile
A warrior's life of lonely dreams of mile upon dusty mile
Dreams of your warmth visions of your eyes
Dragon seed of long gone times heavens priceless prize

A daemon moves upon the earth my lady he seeks for me
The love the life my future my eternity so free
I love you now and ever will to hold your hand in mine
Lady friend my lover kisses so divine

I love you more than life itself beyond honour and my creed
For you my lovely lady are the future I need
Come hold my heart to see it's worth my soul to hear its song
Come my darling eternity is forever and time will not tarry long

CHAPTER 5

Shinning Darkness

Shining Darkness is a compilation of poetry some with a dark side and others with a very upbeat positive side. Those of you who have read my Ancient Warrior poetry may recognize some of the introspection my warrior uses to shape his future or cope with his present.

Shining Darkness

Walk silently in the mysts of time the promise of tomorrow
Dream to see your future against past and forever
Ancient warrior upon this hallowed ground tear upon his cheek
Foe and friend in scattered dance upon the blooded plain

Singing silent songs telling tales of glories past no one hears
Walk my friend with limping gait leave your mark upon the land
Your dreams shatter to silver shards to litter times great sand
Eternity washes them away no trace to be found

Your dragon your daemon your quest remains to pull you forward
A drink a laugh or stumbling dance to mark the time away
Tis dark upon the plain the sky in velvet black
The sounds of merriment reach your soul

In the darkness, they appear to lead you on the way
Friend and Foe from battles past take you by the hand
Drink and shared stories of this day
Enjoy heal your soul for tomorrow the game begins anew

Butterflies

The flutter and gentle touch of butterflies
Gently lapping loves shores heavens cliffs
Eternity and the steps beyond these too are for you
Butterflies love on feathered wings

Wandering in the fields of rainbow colour
Heavens blue nature's gold gossamer clouds
You cleave to me I honour the you
Butterflies gentle seeking the love within

Grass and flower tree and forest
Butterflies in rainbow hue
Seeking the me
Living within the you, Butterflies

Times In the Standing

In the turning twist of loves gentle smile
The Warrior upon his oath does seek your heart
When in the shining night within this winters night
Times move to show the face of love in you tonight

I seek to hear the laughter to see your dancing eyes
Emerald green upon your soul a grand Warriors prize
The gentle curve of your lip your silken skin to touch
These are but a few treasures I love of yours I love so much

I run in the silent dawn knowing you soon will awake
The tiny laugh and stumbling step to seek the morning
We are two but of one for never can we part
You are my soul in all these times the heart of my heart

Winters come and suns do shine here and the next
Forever but an instant within your laughing song
A hearts beat within your arms is eternity plus a day
We the children of those times have forever for our play

Micheal Hopkins

Cast Forth

Cast forth your nets of times uncertainty
Count your catch of fickle eternity
Leave me in my silent musing
Eternity and Time the warrior refusing

Time is but of instant and younger then now
Eternity the sum of time and means nothing
I am the warrior time and eternity my curse
Eternity and time my blessing mixed and unknown

For ten thousand years ten thousand tears
An instant or a forever in whose eyes
I am the warrior you my love the desire
You the ultimate prize, eternity the wedding

Shores of time and freshened waters dew
Seeking and searching and in each time finding you
Oh gods and daemons dragons and clouds
One of all and all are the same when you play eternity's game

Walk upon the trampled plain steel and leather the battle
Wind and clouds and dragons fire honour the duty
And upon the pyre offer up the mirror offer the soul
Crimson daemons, diamond scales, emerald fire

Upon this plain again today upon this life my soul
Battle is waged and times appeased
Eternity ignores for the warrior is victorious
Gods turn to see his face toss the die and move his place

Am I closer upon the seeking of you
Or am I in a game of one I and I alone
The gods moving me in silent rounds
Stop and move no more I say gods be damned

Continued...

I will not play and upon the plains of eternity
I swear my oath and my battle cry, for I will live or I will die
I love you more than life itself
My steel I brandish in mocking salute

Gods' smile tossing the die
Dragons dropping from windblown skye
Diamond scales with emerald eye
Steel talons, baleful cry, dragons from eternity's skye

Shield of leather blessed with loves remembered kiss
Steel edged with loves dew and visions of you
Heart in full-throated cry my love today or I shall die
Upon the plain set dragons in time

Upon the plain step I, upon the plain gods watch
First in a step matched in diamond scale
Then in trot and final run dragons cry
The final battle begun

Clash of steel and diamond scale blood and fire
Stain the plain steel ringing in pure pitched song
Talons ripping wounds drawn long
Steel enters and dragons die, souls dancing free

And in the heavens gods do smile
Peace they say give him peace for the while
Dragons smile and stand aside, You are there by my side
We walk in emerald light eternity's shores

We dance upon the mountains love in valleys below
We sing in the wind and we sing of our soul
We laugh and gods do smile
Yes peace to the warrior peace for the while

Micheal Hopkins

Children of the Dragon

The darkness falls around me the light of joy runs to be no more
Remembrance when sorrow walks the land
Gone truly gone but my mind holds you still, a golden light
The dragons take the dream to keep it holy tight, to savor

Tears have forsaken me, the burning pyre of my need, cold
Heavens chase to bring you back but the shade is sorely cold
Could in my remembrance I embrace you once again, to see
But all the emerald tears you shared these I treasure still

Time the cruel and soulless taskmaster eternity but a wish
I seek in the memory, the merry song of your laughter
Gods do toss the die and man does dance the price
I wish to warm my heart but now there is but ice

You ran with me in daemon times you danced my dragon's songs
But now all that remains are your childish dreams, gods the need
Taken in the hour and taken this gray winter's day, home
I remember your laughter I remember your smile, this my treasure

The walking times of never more the winding roads of then
I will always love you my daughter from now to never end
You live with my heart, smile upon my eyes, mirrors of remembrance
But for now, the dragons cry, the daemon weeps in silence
The warrior moves ahead but times in remembrance forever in his
stead

Courage

I stand the armor before me, the steel in the case
I stand and see the mirror the mirror showing my face
I look to the plains and see the times of now
The dragons and the daemons upon the hills brow

I should or could I or would I need to don
I am a warrior of the best but am I good enough
I should or gods about the armor of my liege
Oh his soul is in the time of god's do I have the strength

I will or could or should I gather in the gear
Should I defend the realm or cower deep in here
The gods are laughing at my plight the times of now
Oh heaven help the warrior when dragons fill the brow

Oh should I put the armor on the steel to uncase
To fight the battle noble or cower in this place
Then the voice of my liege I hear upon the wind
You are the one I have chosen the realm to defend

I take up the armor the steel and the helm
The dragons and the daemons upon this fertile ground
I stand and call the heavens I am the one you see
I am the warrior of the realm, the diamonds, and the sea

Micheal Hopkins

Crimson Vest

The night the skye the heavens in vibrant black
The gods in a silent dream the wish to see you smile
The times the tides the movement of the next the need
The wish the could the would the should the kiss the leaving

The dragon sigh the wish of an emerald tear upon golden scale
The daemon in the crimson vest proper upon the plain
The angel in silk and velvet the dream of another time
The need the smile the kiss the caress the wish

The lady to smile to sigh to bid adieu the warrior to bow
The tides to pull the now to next tomorrow on the rim
He smiles he wishes she sighs he kisses
The gods the heavens he honours, she laughs, he goes

Cruel Eternity

Chasing dreams seeking laughter in the night
Shards of forever but wishes in the sand
Eternity silent traveler time forever in her hand
Warrior tear maiden sigh dragon dream in emerald skye

Songs of remembrance dances on the plain
I seek the falling darkness to see the day again
Times sands pulling urging me ever on
Seas and rivulets kissing my soul this day

Winds in sails of souls filling life while my daemons play
I in the arms of tomorrow think of times before
The next but a shadow holding eternity at bay
The abyss does call in siren song dragons' line its rim

Love or hate, laughter and tears each its song must sing
Gentle touch in falling night dreams on butterfly wings
A flower is my gift to you a kiss my promise dear
Eternity a cruel curse a smile on heavens face

I take you to my promised land of next and evermore
We dance to ancient songs unheard with diamond stars
Stars to light our way, forever within your love but one brief day
Come to seek the merry song of life upon this timeless shore

Micheal Hopkins

Dancing Feet

Shapes and smiles in silent shadow sail on silken seas
Dreams and daemons dragons too do delve the house of man
I walk to seek the ending but find the beginning again
The lady runs to find the fallen to make them whole again

Times seas are eternal the end to never come
Man is a lesser thing gone before he is begun
But the soul lives forever sailing upon the main
And love tells the story to bring them home again

I chase the butterfly to seek the beauty of the wind
You smell the scent of roses wild upon the plain
Dragon's songs and daemons dance to live once before
But could and would you in gentler times move on this oaken floor

I dance to the times of then you dance to my hearts beat
We move the world aside my dear and glide on floating feet
But the beat of then the song of now the future in the rim
Come to taste the nectar dear and begin the dance again

Dragon

Stride and strut and scream and smile
Ride the wave; see the sun, move the cloud
I am the dragon, I am the next
The fires of hell are cold to me, I am the dragon

I pace the earth in silent tread, seeking
I walk the skye in rapid loss, seeking
I hide in the shadows of your heart, seeing
I cannot enter nor leave I am here waiting

The tears you cry are the tears of me
The smile is the cost of my soul
The laughter the meaning of my life
The lies are no part of you or me

Walk in the light as I glide in your shadow
I smile time shudders eternity shies away
I guard and daemons will not come
I am and you are, we can, and love will

Dragons Fire

Nothing, in all that you do
Nothing, of all you desire
Nothing, when eternity is done
Nothing you build and no where you run

Not in the moment
Not in the heart
Not one word
Not one tear, will quench the thirst

Nowhere in time
Future or past
Nothing in now
Nothing will last

The judgment is coming
The punishment due
Only the end, a reward to you
Only in time and only in space

Never upon this jeweled face
The eyes will hold you
The power enfold you
And judgment waits upon his face

Dragon tears to cleanse, making you pure
Dragon tears to wash your stained soul
Dragon tears to soothe
Dragon fires cold blow

Twisted Dreams

In the turning times of never now he walks
The ancient warrior seeking times quiet shore
Friend and foemen laughter and tears known
Forgotten the choices forgotten the dreams

Upon times shore the silent wave's crash
Eternity pulling the past to her womb
He seeks among the silvered shards
Once bright dreams now waste upon the sand

Long lost memory calls to him songs with no sound
With steady step and head held high he walks
Ancient warrior battle scarred and torn
Your soul seeks the coming next peace in the void

The dragon on his right his daemon on the left
Caper dancing upon the dreams
But soft in the distance the light of soft remembrance
An emerald tear upon the quay

Dream again of battles won and foemen all so dear
Your heart calls upon your soul to seek the emerald tear
In the settling darkness filled with light
Sleep upon your dream seek the promise of tomorrow

Ancient warrior cursed in time
Forbidden eternities peace
Trapped in time upon the sand
Dreaming twisted dreams

Micheal Hopkins

Dragons Mirror

She stands before the mirror, the light
She stands and sees the reflection of her
But he stands in the shadows the warrior
And he sees the lady, for a reflection is only that

I am a woman she says of no special talent
The mirror says my vision is true
The warrior smiles and sees the soul the heart
The angle of his view

She finds no joy in what she sees inside
She cannot move the vision the visage aside
He sees the love the glow the smile
The visage is in the perception pray stare for a while

She sees not the joy the love the time
She sees not her affect the gentle eddy in time
He sees the fire the glow the need
She is the joy a lady of the Dragons seed

The power the strength she denies
The warrior sees it all in the depth of her eyes
The time the need the anger the smile
He sees the dragon just idle for the while

I am a warrior you a lady true
The warrior the poet the seer of you
The dragon heart the emerald tear
The need to wash away your selfish fear

To see in the mirror your soul and heart so bright
The need to let your dragons wings move you
Move you in joyous flight
Live and love and angle your mirror

Continued......

For in the perception all you have is here
I am the warrior you heart I see so clear
The soul the love the time
Darling shed your skin of futile fear

Dreams of the Heart

Will the world see me as the dreams of my heart
Or will the world move aside to kill it from the start
I wish and that is my armor I need and that is my sword
The soul senses sees and hears the meaning of the words

Can the world let one have the dreams of the heart
Will the gods know and feel what we knew from the start
Would you care to back away to run from your need
I will stand and face the hopes and live my emerald dreams

The dragons march upon the plain the dust of tattered time
The daemons smile upon the clouds the fluff of wasted dream
I stand and watch you in the mist the shape of things out come
I wait I smile I know you will be the only one

You can feel the heart can hear the soul can see my truth
The only things that the gods do bring is the living proof
You are the one the only need that I have upon the earth
The one you wish is the one you need, I stand before you now

The Lady in His Dreams

And In times of silvered smiles in lands of dragons
The warrior upon the battle plains the lady in his dreams
The Poet walks in silent times knowing his dream is near
The wish of the golden heart, the smile of the dragon's tear

The daemon on the edge of time the troll upon your ear
I see the times are of dreams, silken land the wish I hold
Would you of times of tomorrow dream of yesterday
I seek to hold you close to me a smile my heart does warm

The taste of love the scent of time the feel of you upon my soul
I need and wish, want and hold you ever so close inside
When the wheel makes its turn, when we together hold
Shal we take the chance of forever, and take our dragon ride

Micheal Hopkins

Dreams in Passing

Seek the dream for in the dreaming reality is created
I move to see shadows of what may or may not be a dream
I run to chase a thought to seek a flittering glance of tomorrow
Time is each man's dream for the changing is the same

She moves in silent memory to look in the pool
The moon light upon a silver surface tomorrow is revealed
The wind does gently shoo the vision clear away
And in dreams and wishes there is only who can say

But clouds are a dream that hides a sunny day
And winds are the wishes, which shoo the clouds away
The dragon's dream of leather wings upon an emerald skye
The lady dreams of another day another reason why

The warrior dreams of battles past and due
The poet sits to dream the words, written for only you
And would the times of silver dreams wrapped in emerald tears
Would the wishes of another thought break the bond of new

I can see in the future a dream some would say to you
But can a future of never be or a past of never been
For dreams are the reality that our wishes send
I seek a dream in passing I seek the wish of you

Dreams of Angels

Angel wings daemons smiles maiden sighs
On eternity and the sea of tomorrow it matters not
Crimson suns emerald tear shadows of here and then
Heavens shudder stars go dim angel dreams begin

Walking silent among the rows cast in crystal bright
Angels gaze in silent mirth maidens of the night
Mares and dreams lost souls cry maidens softly sigh
Truth be found in darkness yet to shine its light so pure

Angel dreams and maiden smiles love does endure
I see you on the misty mount wreathed in heavens glow
Emerald fire against the sadness of mans dreams of greed
Hold you close feel the need the wish for the morrow

Holding tight in the storm walking the wire of eternal sorrow
I love you so in deepest truth that shines in darkest night
Angel Dreams move the chords of time ring eternity's chimes
For angel wings and daemons smiles maiden sighs and gods Blue
Skye

Micheal Hopkins

A Gentle Song

The wind blows in gentle song to move my heart this day
The sounds of silence caress my soul to show the way
Of today
The moon upon the willows waters silvery night

I would in times of then and now seek the dragon star
The dreams of times are naught for without the lady fair
The wishes of any soul are nothing unless you are there
I could in the moment see the end but know the truth is here

The wish the caress the silent smile, the need for you I feel
The emerald tears are jewels in heaven gossamer crown
Clouds race the face of god the angles tag along
I can seek to see the laughter, the kiss, the knowing eyes

Emerald Tears Golden Scales

Far in the darkness lays the abyss of my mind
Walled dreams silent screams eternity beyond my grasp
Seeking to see the reason why but fearing an answer still
Ancient warrior tired and worn tattered is his soul

Seeking laughter finding naught but emeralds in the sand
Walk upon this mortal plain following the tracks of man
Facing the sun where battle calls in ancient halls
Shades seek to call me in to join their ethereal band

A dragon seeks to hold my soul to caress the pain away
The breath of fire cleansing pain to live another day
Even in my darkest thoughts in screams of merry song
The golden scales of dragon kind emerald tears stain

Chase your dreams for time cares not what you seek to do
Gods in the silent temples waiting watching laughing still
Ancient warrior treads the earth climb the final hill
Questing seeking fail again such is the fate of man

Forever Our Joy

Shattered times and wanton winds, the change of today
Warriors on the fields at night await the coming day
The dragons move to seek the fire warmth on a chilled night
The foemen stand in silent dread to run the coming fight

I move in shadows once of me but now of another man
The mysts of wonder the mists of rain, secrets of shadowed land
Can in the changing times the seas to walk away
The clouds to soak the heat of love the lady on the quay

Should you see the battle true the fight of man and beast?
The dragons stand in silent rank the daemons await the feast
The lady laughs knowing man the weakness of the beast
Ah my times are here the sand of life the seas upon my feet

Walk with me and see the field, roses where the dew is rich
The shapes of love the songs of heart the souls of those before
And in the distance the mysts do fade, eternity opens its door
Come hold me close and run to time the edge of forever our joy

Laughter in Silence

Standing trapped in times mysts eternity pulls ever forward
Sounds trapped in amber dreams smiles etched on diamond tears
The wish of another to seek the test to move in fettered pace
The dragons stand in silent accord to see your going way

Walk upon the times of now following a silent sound
Sands in time's seas foaming grace, a tear courses smiling face
Winds tear at the corners of his soul, clouds bath the sun
Uphill and down, course never taken, traveled by few seen by all

Wishes are dreams of small desire, love a brilliant passions fire
Laughter a gift, smiles treasures held in love's burning heart
Take the time the step for all that is now is eternity's gift
Mountains become the sand flowing through eternal time

Kindness a blessing tears a cure forever in the moment a life

Micheal Hopkins

Shadow of the Night

Shapes and times shadows in the night
Lovers on the shore the moon within their sight
Winds of tomorrow kiss their face now
The wonder of the moment the dream of the how

Walking in the silence of love upon the sand
The shadows of the next upon the silent land
Would you hold me close my love
To dance in eternal song, life the joy the wonder

Times so very long, a wish I hold within
The need to see you smile a kiss a laugh
Changing moods the long eternal mile
Taking and giving and sharing of the heart

Souls of love entwined the moment just the start
The wonder of your touch the warmth of your skin
The tracing of your laughter now the love begins
The dragon laughs the daemon cries

Lovers in the night
Hope and the promise
The song of just right
A sigh

The Wall

I love the time, the scent, and the dew
I feel you in all that I do
I run to the window and tomorrow I see
The you, the future, the love for me

Moving in the silence of night
Riding the hush of the storm
Taking the chance to open the soul
My heart, my love, my eternal now

I move to you in windswept grace
The stars, the moon, the gods
All stand in silent accord, the love of you
Running to the sound of your heart

Knowing it's you and eager to start
The wall, we are building the wall
Dreams upon dreams
Mortared with love, blessed in sun

Walls of dreams, gates of time
Shining in fast honour the love
We are building the walls of tomorrow
Walls to hold back the sorrow

Time is our toy, eternity our land
The future our golden sand
I love you the Skye of my life
Building the walls against the night

Micheal Hopkins

Dance Softly

Dance softly wake not the fallen
Laugh with no sound for sadness seeks the fore
Walk in the shadows of tomorrow's dreams
Marvel at the silver shards of today's

A warrior needs not hate or anger
Duty, Honour, and loves desire all that matter
The foe but friends of different thought
The dragon's enemies of cowardice

Daemons laugh to see man in futile array
Children mimic and the old envy
Lovers slowly shake their heads
Foeman and Friend seek the game

Warriors march to measured beat
Armor glistens on the plains of never more
Blood soaks to feed the earth
Glorious game hear the heavens roar

Poetry by Micheal Hopkins

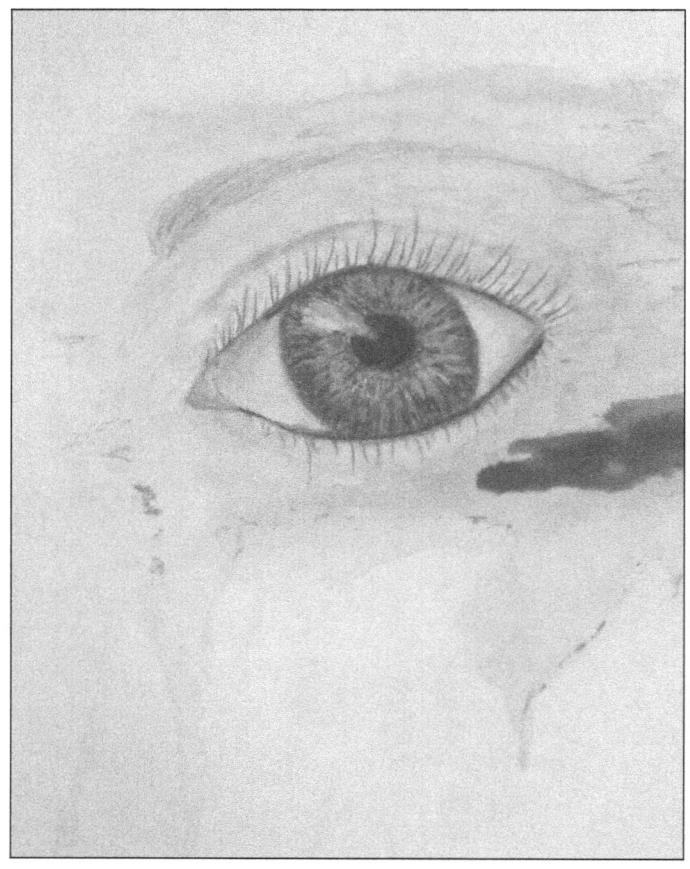

Never-Forget by Carol Hopkins

God the flowers have no right to try and compete with your beauty to me my love, so am sending these flowers to you so that they can see the futility in their actions and return to the second most beautiful of god's creation you the first.

ABOUT

Micheal Hopkins, a Vietnam Veteran is a writer of Poetry, Humorous Fiction, and Nonfiction books. Writing is a passion which must be constantly pursued. Michael sees the humor in the posturing and strutting of humanity taking nothing in life very seriously. Poetry is an outlet although Michael thinks it's the only way to shut his muse up. His poetry tells a tale of an Ancient Warrior.

Several books of Humorous Fiction and Nonfiction are in the works. Besides Micheal's poetry look for his new book Forty Years Behind the Mask will be available in October 2017.

You can read more about Micheal's work at
http://www.shywindcreations.com

www.ingramcontent.com/pod-product-compliance
Lightning Source LLC
Chambersburg PA
CBHW060233180626
46813CB00007B/3068